New Jersey Nets

Jack C. Harris

CREATIVE EDUCATION

Published by Creative Education
123 South Broad Street, Mankato, Minnesota 56001
Creative Education is an imprint of The Creative Company

Designed by Rita Marshall

Photos by: Allsport Photography, Associated Press/Wide World Photos,
Focus on Sports, NBA Photos, UPI/Corbis-Bettmann, and SportsChrome.

Photo page 1: Sam Cassell
Photo title page: Kerry Kittles

Library of Congress Cataloging-in-Publication Data

Harris, Jack C.
New Jersey Nets / Jack C. Harris.
p. cm. — (NBA today)
Summary: A history of the team that began in 1967 as part of the old
American Basketball Association and went through changes in location and
name before becoming officially known as the New Jersey Nets in 1977.
ISBN 0-88682-882-1

1. New Jersey Nets (Basketball team)—Juvenile literature.
[1. New Jersey Nets (Basketball team)—History. 2. Basketball—History.]
I. Title. II. Series: NBA today (Mankato, Minn.)

GV885.52.N37H37 1997   96-51047
796.323'64'09749—dc21

5 4

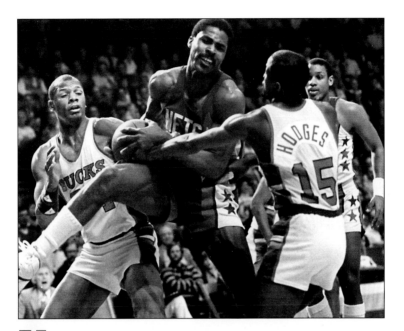

New Jersey is a tiny state; of the 50 states, it ranks 47th in size. In spite of its small size, it is an important state with a long and rich history. As one of the original 13 colonies, New Jersey fought for and won independence from England during the American Revolution. Today, New Jersey has become a center of business, with many of America's biggest companies locating their headquarters in the state. New Jersey is also famous for its scenic farming regions; it proudly bears the "Garden State" nickname.

From colonial times until today, New Jersey residents have worked hard to make their dreams come true. One of

All-Star Buck Williams.

1 9 6 8

Averaging nearly 20 points per game, Levern "Jelly" Tart led the Americans in their first season.

those dreams has been to make the state a center of professional sports. In recent years, two professional football teams, the Giants and the Jets, and a professional hockey club, the Devils, have settled there. But even before pro football and hockey came to New Jersey, the state had a professional basketball team.

New Jersey's basketball club has had an up-and-down history since it was first established in 1967 as part of the old American Basketball Association (ABA). It moved around several times during its first 10 years—from New Jersey to New York and back. It went through several name changes and a league change. But since 1977, the team has been known as the New Jersey Nets and has been a proud member of the National Basketball Association (NBA).

Today, the Nets and coach John Calipari hope to build a basketball powerhouse, starting with a nucleus of Keith Van Horn, Jayson Williams, and young guard Kerry Kittles. If Calipari and the Nets succeed, New Jersey residents could be cheering for one of the NBA's top teams before long.

BLEAK BEGINNINGS

The Nets' story begins with the formation of the American Basketball Association on February 1, 1967. Although this trouble-filled league lasted only nine years, it added much to the history of professional basketball. Numerous exceptional players first starred in the ABA, and the league pioneered such innovations as the three-point shot, the 30-second clock, and the red-white-and-blue basketball.

Derrick Coleman, a Nets leader.

*Reserve guard Bob
Lloyd hit 43 free
throws in a row,
a league record.*

Unfortunately, the ABA was also known for its slipshod organization and large debts.

A club called the New Jersey Americans, coached by Max Zaslofsky, was an original member of the ABA. The club played in Teaneck, New Jersey, just across the Hudson River from New York City. Its home was a gloomy U.S. military building known as the Teaneck Armory.

It was not a promising beginning. Many potential fans in the area didn't even know how to find Teaneck. Also, the roof of the armory often leaked, and at least one of the club's home games had to be postponed because of rain. Yet some of that New Jersey determination must have rubbed off on the Americans, because Zaslofsky's club managed to compile a 36–42 record its first year—good enough to tie for fourth place in its division.

But the next season New Jersey lost its team entirely. The club changed its name to the New York Nets and moved into the Commack Arena on Long Island. Management said that the move would boost the team's fortunes, but it didn't work out that way. The Nets suffered through a disappointing 17–61 season, and only about a thousand people showed up to watch each home game played in the rickety arena.

Luckily, a wealthy businessman named Roy Boe turned things around. He purchased the team and lured two talented young NBA players to the Nets—guard Bill Melchionni and forward Sonny Dove. The two new regulars joined with veteran Levern Tart to lead the Nets to a 39–47 record in 1969–70—a 23-game improvement over the previous year. The future was beginning to look brighter.

Nets fans had even more reason for optimism as the 1970–71 season began. They moved to the Island Garden Arena on New York's Long Island, an improvement over the old Commack Arena. Then colorful college coach Lou Carnesecca took over the reins of the team. Carnesecca was a real showman. He paced up and down the sidelines during the games, hollering at the referees, pulling his hair in frustration. The fans loved it.

Accurate ABA shooter Billy Paultz hit 52 percent of his field-goal attempts.

The Nets also acquired the team's first superstar when they signed former NBA scoring champ Rick Barry, an offensive wonder. Barry moved across the court gracefully; he could pull up for long-range jumpers or drive to the hoop with equal success. "I rank Rick as the greatest and most productive offensive forward ever to play the game," said Hall of Famer Bill Sharman, Barry's former coach with the NBA's Golden State Warriors.

As great as his outside shooting was, Barry was even more famous for shooting free throws the old-fashioned, underhanded way. Many people thought the shot looked odd, but they couldn't argue with Barry's free-throw success rate of nearly 90 percent during the season. Barry averaged an impressive 29.4 points per game, and he became the first Net named to the ABA's All-League Team.

Carnesecca's coaching and the fine play of Barry, center Billy "The Whopper" Paultz, forward Manny Leeks, and rookie guard John Roche helped the Nets compile their best record yet, 40–44. Despite the improvement, Roy Boe's team

Julius Erving, one of basketball's finest.

Scoring champion Rick Barry.

still lost an estimated $2.5 million that year. How long could he keep the franchise going?

1 9 7 2

Using his unusual underhanded style, Rick Barry sank 641 of 730 free-throw attempts.

THE DOCTOR COMES TO OPERATE

Roy Boe decided to put everything on the line. His decisions over the next few years helped turn the Nets into a big winner both on the court and at the ticket office. This success paved the way for the club to join the more established National Basketball Association.

Boe started by moving the team to its fourth home, the spacious Nassau Veterans Memorial Coliseum in Uniondale, New York. There, in 1971–72, the Nets compiled their first winning record, 44–40. They even reached the final round of the ABA playoffs, falling to the Indiana Pacers four games to two in the league championship series. Rick Barry averaged more than 31 points per game and topped the league in free-throw shooting, while Bill Melchionni led the ABA in assists. The Nets seemed to be on the verge of greatness.

The following year, however, the club fell quickly after a federal judge ruled that Rick Barry had to return to his old NBA club, the Warriors. Without Barry, the Nets could compile only a 30–54 record in the 1972–73 season.

But Roy Boe had a few more tricks up his sleeve. He brought in former NBA star guard Kevin Loughery to coach the club. Then he signed a "super superstar" named Julius Erving to control the offense and thrill the fans.

Erving was nicknamed "Dr. J" for the way he "operated" on the court. The 6-foot-6 Erving was as perfect a basketball player as the game has ever seen. He moved with astonishing speed and grace. When he jumped, he seemed to defy gravity, maneuvering in space, sailing over opponents—much like Michael Jordan did years later.

Nets center Billy Paultz often watched Dr. J in amazement. "Julius has this motion where he just hangs up there and levitates up and down, up and down," he said. "I know that just can't be, but I swear it's what he does."

"Doc goes up and never comes down," said astonished teammate Bill Melchionni.

The Nets soared during the 1973–74 season, Dr. J's first with the club, winning 55 regular-season games—an unbelievable 25 victories more than the previous season. They topped off the year by routing the Utah Stars in the championship round of the playoffs to win their first ABA title.

Dr. J led the league in scoring with an average of 27.4 points per game and was a standout on defense as well, ranking third in both steals and blocked shots. He was a runaway choice for the ABA's Most Valuable Player award.

Two seasons later, the Nets staged a replay of that magical year. They duplicated their 55–29 record, with Dr. J again leading the league in scoring. He then led the club to a second ABA championship. The Nets were not only making headlines, but they were finally making money as well.

1 9 7 3

Even without Rick Barry around, Bill Melchionni won his third straight ABA assists crown.

NEW LEAGUE, NEW HOME, NEW STAR

The big story of the 1975–76 ABA season wasn't the Nets' success, however. The year also marked the end of the league's brief history. As the ABA and NBA merged to form one league, four ABA teams survived to become new

NBA franchises—the Indiana Pacers, Denver Nuggets, San Antonio Spurs, and New York Nets.

1 9 7 6

Julius Erving won his third ABA scoring title and a third MVP award.

That was the good news for Nets fans, but their excitement was short-lived. Rumors began circulating about Dr. J's status with the new NBA Nets. Erving wanted the Nets to renegotiate his contract and increase his salary, but Boe couldn't afford the extra money. In the end, a trade was the only agreement Boe and Erving could reach. Dr. J packed his bags and headed to the Philadelphia 76ers.

Without Erving, the outlook for the team in its first NBA season wasn't very bright. "How could anyone do this to us?" Nets guard John Williamson said after hearing about the trade. "Our season is over already." Williamson turned out to be right. The club plummeted in 1976–77, compiling a 22–60 record, the worst in the league.

Before the 1977–78 season began, Boe moved his team once more. This time they headed back to their first home state. On September 12, 1977, the New Jersey Nets were officially born, and what they needed was a new superstar. Roy Boe believed he had found one when he signed Bernard King, a talented rookie forward from the University of Tennessee, to a Nets contract.

Bernard King did everything he could to turn the Nets around in his rookie year. He averaged 24.2 points and 9.5 rebounds per game and was named to the league's All-Rookie team. "Bernard King is a scoring machine," said Red Holzman, a former Knicks coach. "What impresses me is how he shoots with such quickness and accuracy. Other teams overplay him and try to deny him the ball. But he keeps scoring." King's efforts weren't enough, though, to

Powerful guard John Williamson.

keep the club from recording the worst win-loss mark in the league (24–58) for the second straight year.

King kept up his fine play the next season, and this time he had some help. John Williamson, who dubbed himself "Super John," returned to New Jersey after a season with the Indiana Pacers. Williamson edged King out as the club's top scorer, and rookie point guard Eddie Jordan provided solid leadership that paced the Nets to a 37–45 record and their first berth in the NBA playoffs. Unfortunately, they came up against Dr. J and the 76ers in the first round, and were quickly wiped out.

After that, the Nets lost their momentum and returned to the cellar in their division. One of the club's biggest problems was turnover. Players quickly came and went. Even team star Bernard King was traded. By the 1980–81 season, the Nets' roster was made up mainly of journeymen and youngsters, including Darwin Cook, Mike Gminski, Mike O'Koren, and Cliff Robinson.

All the player changes were too much for Coach Loughery. In December 1980, he resigned, and the coaching tasks were given to his assistant, Bob MacKinnon, for the remainder of the miserable 24–58 season.

The next year another new coach—Larry Brown—was at the helm. Brown had achieved an exceptional record in the college ranks at UCLA, and also as coach of the Denver Nuggets in both the ABA and NBA. "Larry has some bulldog in him," said MacKinnon. "He's a very determined guy who not only expects, but usually gets, 100 percent from his players. He will be successful."

1 9 7 7

Bernard King set Nets rookie records in scoring and field goals during his inaugural season.

MacKinnon's prediction of success came true during Brown's first year. The club improved by an amazing 20 wins, finishing with a 44–38 record for the 1981–82 season. There were three main reasons for the change: (1) Brown's ability to inspire his players; (2) the Nets' move to a new home, the Brendan Byrne Arena in East Rutherford; and (3) the presence of a new star, a 21-year-old rookie named Charles "Buck" Williams. Williams provided ferocious rebounding and a solid inside-scoring touch that earned him the NBA's Rookie of the Year award and even some votes for league's Most Valuable Player.

Kevin Porter's 29 assists in a game against Houston set a record that stood for 10 years.

Former Nets star Rick Barry, by then a basketball analyst on television, named Buck Williams to his "all-lunch-pail team." What Barry meant was that Williams came to work hard every night and did his battling under the boards, where the job is toughest. "He's consistent, hardworking, and tough," Barry added. "Every team should be blessed with a Buck Williams." Nets fans agreed and were certain the hustling young star would lead their favorite club back to the heights it had achieved in the ABA.

Optimism reached a fever pitch the next season. The former cellar-dweller Nets challenged the NBA's leaders with a 49–33 record in 1982–83. Everything seemed fine in New Jersey—until the last two weeks of the season. Then it was learned that Coach Brown was working out a contract to leave the Nets the next year for the University of Kansas. Angry and disappointed, the Nets' owners asked Brown to

Menacing center Sam Bowie (pages 18–19).

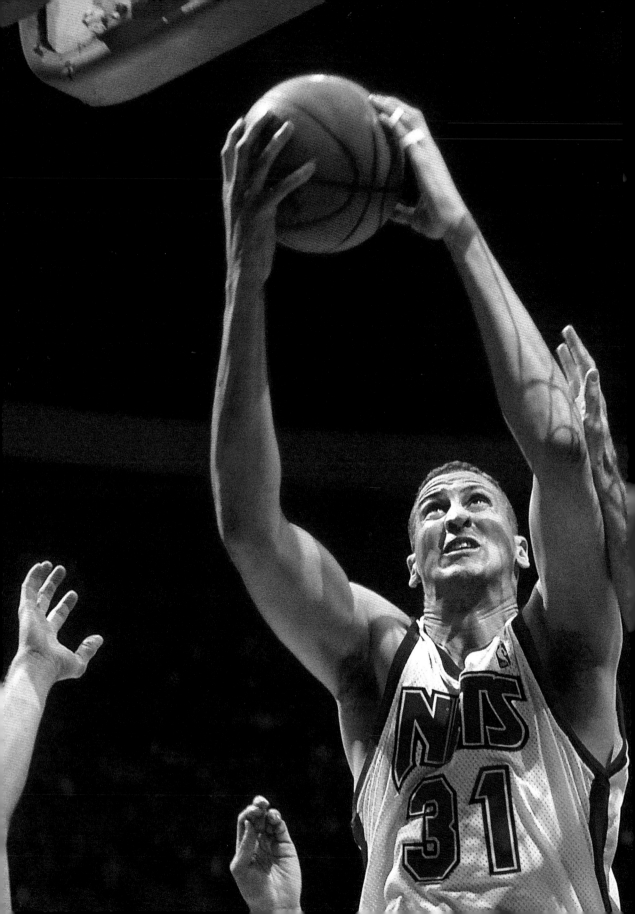

resign immediately. The coach's departure shook up the players. They won only two of their last six games and were quickly eliminated from the playoffs.

Stan Albeck took over the club as the 1983–84 season began. "He runs things the way they should be run," said Nets reserve guard Foots Walker. "We're planning on running to the playoffs and maybe even further," said Albeck.

Buck Williams was the Nets' scoring leader with an average of 17 points per game.

The new coach put the ball into the hands of three-time All-Star guard Otis Birdsong and super point guard Micheal Ray Richardson. Albert King—Bernard's younger brother—provided additional offensive help. Albeck also prodded center Darryl Dawkins, who had a reputation for being lazy, to become a rebounding and scoring force. And, of course, there was Buck Williams. Williams averaged 15.7 points per game and, for the third year in a row, grabbed more than 1,000 rebounds.

The Nets ended the 1983–84 regular season with a 19–8 stretch run that rolled them right into the playoffs, just as Coach Albeck had predicted. Then, in a major upset, they wiped out the defending NBA champion Philadelphia 76ers in the first round. Though the Nets fell to the Milwaukee Bucks in the Eastern Conference semifinals, Albeck felt encouraged. He told reporters, "We went further than anyone predicted we would, but not nearly as far as we're capable of going. The best thing that came out of this season was a new feeling of confidence. From now on, you'll probably hear Nets players talking more about the NBA championship. These guys really believe they can go all the way now, whether anyone else believes it or not."

In 1984–85, anticipation of a championship season was high among Nets fans and players. But the club's hopes were plagued by injuries. Everything from broken legs to sprained ankles kept Dawkins, King, O'Koren, and Birdsong out of the lineup for much of the season. Buck Williams and Micheal Ray Richardson played even harder than usual to make up for the missing wounded. Under their leadership, the Nets managed a winning season (42–40), earning a berth in the 1985 playoffs. Williams became the first forward in history to snag 1,000 or more rebounds in every one of his first four seasons in the NBA. Meanwhile, Richardson led the league in steals and made the All-Star team.

Darryl Dawkins's thunderous dunks helped rank him among league leaders in shooting percentages.

But the frustrating season had been too much for Albeck, who resigned at year's end. He was followed by two other coaches during the next four seasons—Dave Wohl and Willis Reed. Neither was able to improve the team's fortunes. Injuries, personal problems, and poor draft picks sent New Jersey spiraling to the bottom of the NBA. Floor general Micheal Ray Richardson tested positive for drug use and was suspended from the league. Without Richardson's leadership, the club's record fell to 39–43 in 1985–86, and the team was quickly eliminated in the first round of the playoffs.

The next season, the Nets banked their hopes on a rookie point guard named Dwayne "the Pearl" Washington. But neither the Pearl nor the Nets ever got on track, and the team failed to make the playoffs for the first time in six years. In fact, the club's 24–58 record was the second worst in its NBA

All-Star Otis Birdsong.

history. New players Roy Hinson and Orlando Woolridge were brought in with high hopes over the next couple of years, but both spent as much time on the injured reserve list as on the court. The Nets failed to make the playoffs in 1987–88 and again in 1988–89.

Then veteran NBA coach Bill Fitch took over the Nets' reins. Fitch became the club's 11th coach in 22 years. New Jersey fans knew Fitch was a proven winner—he had led the Celtics to an NBA title in the early 1980s—but they wondered if he could make the Nets winners too.

For the third time in his career, Micheal Ray Richardson led the NBA in steals.

"You're only as good as your talent," the new coach stated, analyzing his job. "Our first task will be kicking the losing habit. It's not impossible."

Fitch looked at his available talent and realized that it was pretty shaky. The roster included veterans Buck Williams and Roy Hinson at forward, with youngster Chris Morris backing them up. Veteran point guards Lester Conner and John Bagley were solid, but not spectacular. The team's best scorer was second-year guard Dennis Hopson, but injuries and poor defensive play were holding him back. The club lacked a strong rebounder and scorer at center. Worst of all, because of an earlier trade, there would be no first-round pick in the 1989 college draft. Fitch faced a tough task.

The coach solved two of his biggest problems with one controversial move. He sacrificed longtime star Buck Williams to Portland for 7-foot-1 center Sam Bowie and the Trail Blazers' number one pick. The Nets then used their new first-round draft pick to acquire Mookie Blaylock from the University of Oklahoma. Blaylock was famous in college for his fast feet on offense and even faster hands on defense.

*Mike Gminski's
.906 free-throw
percentage ranked
fourth in the NBA.*

Young center Chris Dudley was also obtained during the season to back up Bowie, who had a history of injuries.

The three new players helped Fitch change the sluggish Nets into a running team. Bowie, in particular, added two skills the team had been missing in the middle: shot-blocking and passing. "Bowie is simply one of the best passing big men in the game," said Rick Barry. Bowie amazed some of the experts by playing almost the entire season without injury and averaging more than 14 points and 10 rebounds per game. He was named the league's Comeback Player of the Year. When Bowie did go down late in the year, Dudley provided solid rebounding and defense.

Overall, however, Fitch's moves didn't seem to be working. Nets fans, who were already angry at the loss of Buck Williams, grew even more angry when the club suffered through a nightmare campaign (17–65) in Fitch's first year with the team.

Reporter Mark Weber of *The Star-Ledger* in Newark, summarizing the Nets' history, noted, "Since being absorbed by the NBA in 1976, they have advanced past the first round of the playoffs just once and haven't played a post-season game since 1986. In each of the last four seasons, they have failed to win more than 26 games."

REBUILDING IN THE 1990s

The Nets' high expectations continued to meet with lackluster results. The Nets' brightest season of the decade was 1993–94, when Derrick Coleman and Kenny Anderson were led by veteran coach Chuck Daly, who had won two

NBA championships with the Detroit Pistons and had coached the 1992 Olympic Dream Team to a gold medal. In Daly's second year at the helm, the Nets finished 45–37—the club's second-best record since entering the NBA.

But contractual disputes, injuries, and player turnover held the team down. The Nets of the 1990s have never made it past the first round of the playoffs, and their failed hopes are symbolized by the tragedy of Drazen Petrovic.

Petrovic was one of several talented European players who entered the NBA in the late 1980s and early 1990s. Petrovic played two years of college ball for Notre Dame before he was drafted by the Portland Trail Blazers, where he began playing in 1989. He established himself as one of the NBA's best scoring guards, building up one of the top points-per-minute ratios. He bolstered his reputation internationally when he won two Olympic silver medals—one for Yugoslavia and one for Croatia. Petrovic's Olympic teams were bested for the gold medal by only the U.S. Dream Teams.

At 28 years old, Petrovic had played two full seasons in New Jersey and was coming off his best season (1992–93) in the NBA, having led the Nets with 22.3 points per game. After the Nets lost in the playoffs, Petrovic went back to Europe to play for the Croatian national team in the off-season. He was driving to visit his girlfriend in Germany following a tournament game in Poland when a semi hit his car head-on, killing him instantly. The next season, the Nets retired Petrovic's jersey—number 3—in his honor.

"You couldn't have wanted a better teammate," said coach Daly of Petrovic. "He was very talented. He played very hard and was able to lead by his example."

1 9 9 3

Forward Chris Morris, in his fifth season with the Nets, led the team in steals with 144.

Long-range shooter Kendall Gill (pages 26–27).

The Nets honored the late Drazen Petrovic by retiring his jersey number 3.

After the loss of Petrovic, the Nets hunkered down and committed to long-term rebuilding—a direction made most evident by the hiring of John Calipari as head coach in 1996–97. Calipari had turned around a mediocre basketball program at the University of Massachusetts, coaching the team into the NCAA Final Four. In a controversial move, he left a successful college program because he was given the leeway and the time to build a winner in the pro ranks in New Jersey.

"I'm not trying to be GM or player-personnel director. I just want to have final say on who is on my team. When that came about with the Nets and they gave me a five-year contract, which gives me time to do it the right way—slowly, not too slowly, but slowly enough where we are not trying to quick-fix things—I took it. We're going to do it right and build a base."

Calipari expected that base to include 7-foot-2 center Shawn Bradley. Bradley was drafted out of Brigham Young by the Philadelphia 76ers in 1993, but never played as well as the 76ers expected. When he was traded to New Jersey in 1995, he began to turn things around. In his first year as a Net, Bradley was second in the league in blocked shots, and became the first player in NBA history to record double-figure blocks in two consecutive games on two separate occasions.

"Shawn Bradley is 26 years old," said Calipari. "After two years of playing in our system—knowing what we're looking for and getting tougher—he'll be a 7-foot-6 guy [pulling his own] weight. Then, we'll go out and get an All-Star to go with him."

With Bradley and teammates Kendall Gill, Jayson

Williams, and Kerry Kittles, Calipari had hopes of bringing success to New Jersey the way he brought it to a previously unheralded University of Massachusetts team. Kittles added consistent scoring punch throughout his rookie season, proving that the accolades he received as an All-American at Villanova were on the mark. In high school, Kittles had been named Mr. Basketball of Louisiana, and as the first-round draft choice of the Nets, he may get that title back again.

Shawn Bradley made 12 blocks in a game against Toronto—an individual record.

"He really has some stuff to his game," said coach Calipari of Kittles. "He's a great athlete."

"I feed off my teammates just as I did in college," Kittles said of his style of play. Kittles, whose trademark is wearing one short sock and one long sock, feels that his game, while consistent in style, has developed. "I think my versatility in college has translated into my versatility in the NBA."

As the 1996–97 season progressed, Bradley did have a major impact on the Nets, though not in the way Calipari had expected. On February 7, 1997, Bradley was part of the biggest trade to take place in the NBA in more than 30 years. He and teammates Khalid Reeves, Ed O'Bannon, and Robert Pack were sent to the Dallas Mavericks in exchange for center Eric Montross, forwards Chris Gatling and George Mc-Cloud (who days later was traded to the Lakers), and guards Sam Cassell and Jim Jackson.

"This is a deal of tremendous magnitude for both teams," said Calipari of the trade. "Jim Jackson has the potential to be one of the true stars in the NBA. Chris Gatling was a member of the 1997 All-Star team, and Sam Cassell has two championship rings. We feel we have increased the strength of the roster both in the present and for the future."

Top sixth man Jayson Williams.

All-around sensation Jim Jackson.

Though Cassell and the 6-foot-10 Gatling were having breakthrough seasons in Dallas, the top prospect for the Nets was fifth-year player Jim Jackson. With a career scoring average of 20.4 points, Jackson had already received wide praise around the NBA. But he didn't stay long in New Jersey. In yet another big trade, Jackson, along with center Eric Montross and two draft picks, was sent to the Philadelphia 76ers. The Nets, in turn, received number two draft pick Keith Van Horn, a high-scoring forward from the University of Utah, and three veterans, center Michael Cage, swingman Lucious Harris, and forward Don MacLean.

"We looked at him as another piece of the puzzle," said Calipari of the 6-foot-10 Van Horn, who led Utah in scoring in each of his four years at the university. "We're not looking at Keith Van Horn as our savior. We're looking at him, as we build this team, as a player who adds great versatility." Calipari hopes his new lineup will be the foundation for success in New Jersey. Fans may have to wait another season or two before he brings total success to New Jersey, but the wait should be worthwhile. If their latest work has been any indicator, the Nets will be among the NBA's top teams sooner rather than later.

"It's the body in the uniform," Calipari said. "It's not the Nets' logo. It's not the Nets' uniform. It's the players within. That's what we're looking to build."